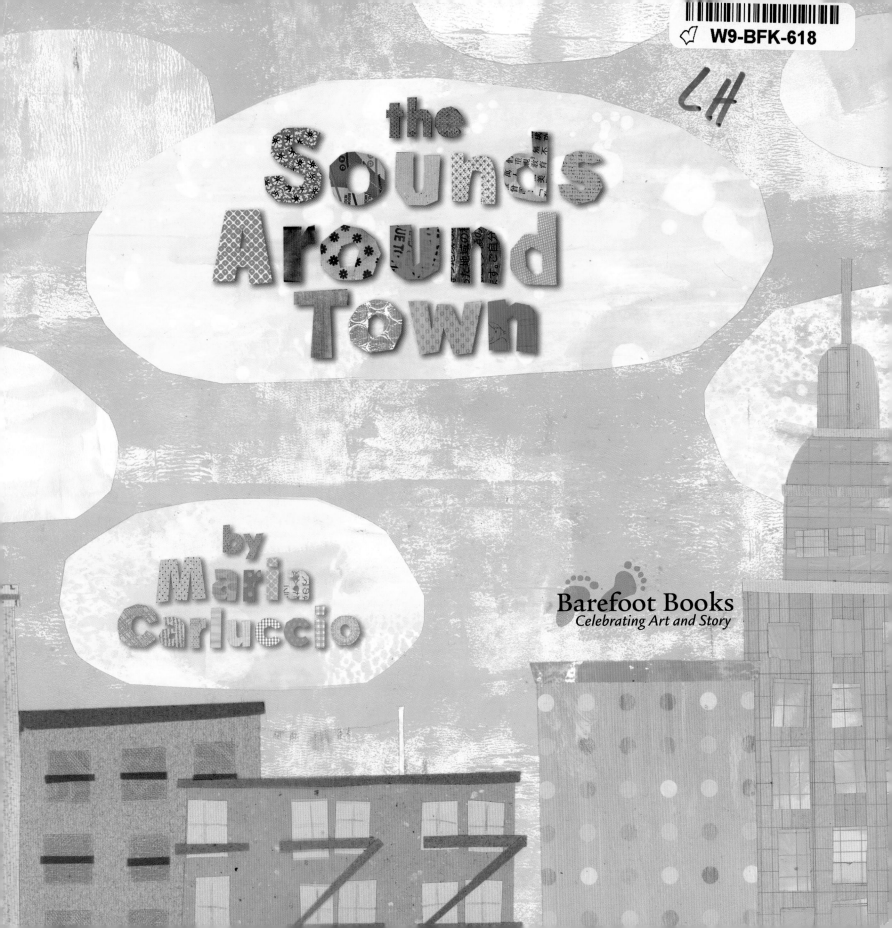

the Sounds Around Town

by Maria Carluccio

Barefoot Books
Celebrating Art and Story

When the sun comes up, the birds start to sing,

tweet, tweet, tweet — a new day begins.

tick-tock,
tick-tock

purr, purr

Morning with Daddy is lots of fun.

We eat up our breakfast, yum, yum, yum.

snap, snap

There's a chill outside; Mommy puts on my cap.

She closes my jacket, snap, snap, snap.

The streets are filled with a wonderful song.
Music is everywhere, ding, ding, dong.

swish, swish

eet,
eet

We stop at the park to feed the ducks and the fish.

High on the swings, I go swish, swish, swish.

yum, yum

ooh, aah

crinkle,
crinkle

lick, lick

The open-air market is our favorite stop.

Look at the vegetables, chop, chop, chop.

ding, dong

clatter, clatter

We join our friends for a lunchtime break.

Here's the sugar, *shake, shake, shake.*

squeak, squeak

vroom, vroom

au revoir!

The children at school will be going home soon.

There's the yellow bus, vroom, vroom, vroom.

Now Daddy gives me a bath in my tub.
I splish, splash in the water, rub-a-dub-dub.

pop, pop

whooosh!

squeak, squeak

splish, splash

Bubbles

purr, purr

The moon is above me, shining full and bright,
It's time to go to sleep now. Sweet dreams and good night!

To my little Maja — M. C.

Barefoot Books
2067 Massachusetts Ave
Cambridge, MA 02140

Text and illustrations copyright © 2008 by Maria Carluccio
Title lettering by Maria Carluccio
The moral right of Maria Carluccio to be identified as the author and illustrator of this work has been asserted

First published in the United States of America by Barefoot Books, Inc in 2008
This paperback edition published in 2011
All rights reserved

Graphic design by Judy Linard, London
Color separation by Grafiscan, Verona
Printed in China on 100% acid-free paper by Printplus, Ltd

This book was typeset in Freedom CW Heavy, Avenir 85 Heavy and Kidprint MT Bold
The illustrations were created by collaging painted papers as well as found papers

ISBN 978-1-84686-430-8

Library of Congress Cataloging-in-Publication Data is available under LCCN 2007025044

1 3 5 7 9 8 6 4 2